Dear Parents:

Congratulations! Your child is taking the first steps on an exciting journey. The destination? Independent reading!

STEP INTO READING® will help your child get there. The program offers five steps to reading success. Each step includes fun stories and colorful art or photographs. In addition to original fiction and books with favorite characters, there are Step into Reading Non-Fiction Readers, Phonics Readers and Boxed Sets, Sticker Readers, and Comic Readers—a complete literacy program with something to interest every child.

Learning to Read, Step by Step!

Ready to Read   Preschool–Kindergarten
• big type and easy words • rhyme and rhythm • picture clues
For children who know the alphabet and are eager to begin reading.

Reading with Help   Preschool–Grade 1
• basic vocabulary • short sentences • simple stories
For children who recognize familiar words and sound out new words with help.

Reading on Your Own   Grades 1–3
• engaging characters • easy-to-follow plots • popular topics
For children who are ready to read on their own.

Reading Paragraphs   Grades 2–3
• challenging vocabulary • short paragraphs • exciting stories
For newly independent readers who read simple sentences with confidence.

Ready for Chapters   Grades 2–4
• chapters • longer paragraphs • full-color art
For children who want to take the plunge into chapter books but still like colorful pictures.

STEP INTO READING® is designed to give every child a successful reading experience. The grade levels are only guides; children will progress through the steps at their own speed, developing confidence in their reading.

Remember, a lifetime love of reading starts with a single step!

Step into Reading, Random House, and the Random House colophon are registered trademarks of Random House LLC.

Visit us on the Web!
StepIntoReading.com
randomhouse.com/kids

Educators and librarians, for a variety of teaching tools, visit us at
RHTeachersLibrarians.com

ISBN 978-0-553-49856-1 (trade) — ISBN 978-0-553-49857-8 (lib. bdg.) —
ISBN 978-0-553-49858-5 (ebook)

Printed in the United States of America   10 9 8 7 6 5 4 3 2 1

JULIUS JR.™

HOWDY-DOODLE-DOO!

Adapted by Mary Tillworth

Illustrated by Jennifer Song

Random House 🏠 New York

Farm day!

Sheree says hello!

The farmer says

howdy-doodle-doo!

The farmer is a rooster.

The farmer wants
to go to town.
But he has
many chores!

Water the flowers.

Pick the berries.

Mind the chickens!

Sheree will help!

The farmer gives Sheree
the keys to the farm.

He goes to town.

Oh, no!
The chickens run
out of the coop!

Sheree chases
the chickens.
They are too fast!

Sheree calls her friends.
She asks for help.

Sheree's friends arrive.
They are ready
to work!

Ping and Clancy
water the flowers.

Worry Bear picks berries
and puts them
in a basket.

Where are the chickens?
They are in the pond.

Julius makes

a chicken scoop.

Julius catches
the chickens!
He puts them
in the chicken coop.

Uh-oh!

Two missing chickens!

The farmer comes back.
Sheree and Julius tell him
about the missing chickens.

The farmer calls
the chickens.

No chickens.
The farmer's voice
is too quiet!

Julius makes
a tool for the farmer!

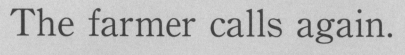

The farmer calls again.
Now he is loud.

The two chickens
hear him.
They return!

Teamwork saves the day!